THE JUPITER TWINS

SCOUT TRIP TO SATURN

BY JEFF DINARDO
ILLUSTRATED BY DAVE CLEGG

RED CHAIR
PRESS

Funny Bone Books

and Funny Bone Readers are produced and published by
Red Chair Press LLC   PO Box 333   South Egremont, MA 01258-0333
www.redchairpress.com

About the Author

Jeff Dinardo's books are filled with humor and silliness that captures a child's imagination. When not writing, Jeff runs a successful design firm specializing in textbooks for use in classrooms from K-8.

About the Artist

Dave Clegg lives and works on a small horse farm in north Georgia with his wife Lyn. All of Dave's work is done digitally on his computer. When he is not drawing, he can be found creating songs with his guitar or making robot sculptures!

Publisher's Cataloging-In-Publication Data
Names: Dinardo, Jeffrey. | Clegg, Dave, illustrator.

Title: The Jupiter twins. Book 3, Scout trip to Saturn / by Jeff Dinardo ; illustrated by Dave Clegg.
Other Titles: Scout trip to Saturn

Description: South Egremont, MA : Red Chair Press, [2018] | Series: Funny bone books. First chapters | Interest age level: 005-007. | Summary: "Trudy and Tina are best friends. They are also twins. Trudy loves adventure and Tina is happy to go along for the ride--as long as it is a smooth ride! It's time for the Troop 552 sleepover on Saturn. Get ready for the chills and thrills of camping out for the first time. First Chapters books are easy introductions to exploring longer text."--Provided by publisher.

Identifiers: LCCN 2017934025 | ISBN 978-1-63440-251-4 (library hardcover)
| ISBN 978-1-63440-255-2 (paperback) | ISBN 978-1-63440-259-0 (ebook)

Subjects: LCSH: Twins--Juvenile fiction. | Saturn (Planet)--Juvenile fiction. | Outer space--Exploration--Juvenile fiction. | Camping--Juvenile fiction. | CYAC: Twins--Fiction. | Saturn (Planet)--Fiction. | Outer space--Exploration--Fiction. | Camping--Fiction.

Classification: LCC PZ7.D6115 Jus 2018 (print) | LCC PZ7.D6115 (ebook) | DDC [E]--dc23

Printed in Canada

102017 1P FRNS18

CONTENTS

MEET THE CHARACTERS

TRUDY

TINA

MS. BICKLEBLORB

POLLY

 OFF WE GO

All the girls in Jupiter Troop 552 were ready to go. They had their sleeping bags, tents, and supplies. Ms. Bickleblorb, their teacher, was also the troop's scout leader. "Everyone on board," she said. "Next stop, Saturn."

"Wait for us!" yelled Tina and Trudy as they hurried to join the others.

They were twins and did everything together.

"Just in time girls," said Ms. Bickleblorb.

The space bus blasted off and flew to the far side of Saturn. This was the troop's first time camping and they were excited.

"I hope we meet some aliens," said Trudy.

"Goodness, I hope not," said Tina.

Everyone got to work setting up their tents and were soon ready for inspection.

Ms. Bickleblorb looked at each one. "Excellent," she said to one scout. "Perfectly done," she said to another.

When she got to Polly's tent she stopped.

There was no tent, just Polly.

"Where's your tent?" Ms. Bickleblorb asked.

"I think I left it at home," Polly said sadly. She looked like she might cry.

"It's no problem," said Ms. Bickleblorb as she looked around. "Tina and Trudy have a large tent so you can stay with them."

Polly smiled at them. She was always trying to hang out with the twins.

"Oh no," said Trudy. "We get stuck
with *Pesky* Polly."

"I think she is just lonely," said Tina,
who waved for Polly to join them.

That night the girls cooked on
the campfire. They sang songs.
They played games.

Then it was time to tell stories.

Ms. Bickleblorb told a silly story
about Ice Giants on Neptune.

Everyone laughed.

"Does anyone else have a story?"
Ms. Bickleblorb asked.

All the scouts looked at each other.

Polly slowly raised her hand. "I know
a spooky story I can tell," she said.

"Excellent," said Ms. Bickleblorb as
she made room for Polly in front of the
campfire.

"I bet this will be boring," whispered
Trudy.

"Quiet," said Tina.

"It was a dark and stormy night at the scout campground," Polly began.

Trudy yawned.

Tina nudged her sister. "Be polite."

Polly continued.

"The campers were huddled near the fire to stay warm. The strong wind drowned out all sounds so they did not hear the mysterious creature dragging itself along the ground. The beast slowly made its way toward the unsuspecting campers."

Trudy and Tina hugged each other.

Polly continued.

"*A clawed hand grabbed one of the campers. The girl screamed and saw it was the terrible two-headed hairy monster!*"

All the campers seemed nervous.

"Yikes!" shouted Tina.

"I think that is enough scary stories for one night," Ms. Bickleblorb said. "It's bed time anyway, so everyone get in your tents."

"Wonderful," said Trudy. "Now I'll
never get to sleep.

Polly brought in her sleeping bag and
all three of them settled in for the night.

Soon Tina and Polly were asleep.

But not Trudy. She sat up in her
sleeping bag staring out into the
darkness.

Trudy's eyes started getting droopy but
she suddenly heard the sound of footsteps
outside. She looked at her sister, but Tina
was still asleep. So was Polly.

Trudy heard more noises.

The footsteps were getting closer.

"Jumping Jupiter," she said to herself.

Trudy looked around and grabbed her flashlight. She wasn't going to let some monster grab her.

3 THE MONSTER

Trudy slowly climbed outside her tent and turned on her flashlight.

"Is anyone out here?" she asked.

Trudy saw a shape come out of the bushes. It was tall..... it was hairy..... it had two heads..... and it had sharp claws.

"It's a two-headed, hairy monster!" Trudy yelled.

Just then, Polly came running out of the tent. "I'll save you!" she yelled. Polly tried to tackle the monster by the legs.

But the monster just giggled. "That tickles," it said.

All the campers came out of their tents to see what was going on.

The creature with two heads spoke.

"Hey, are you the scout troop from Jupiter?" one head said.

"We heard you were coming and we were all so excited to meet you," said the other head.

Ms. Bickleblorb smiled. "Yes we are the scout troop from Jupiter," she said. "Who are you?"

"I'm Zoe," said one head.

"And I'm Violet," said the other. "But my friends call me Vi."

"We're Saturn Scouts!" they both said. "We came over to see if you wanted to join our group for a sing-a-long."

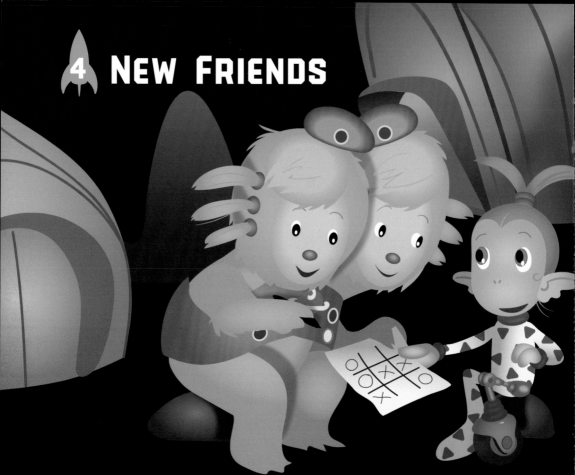

4 NEW FRIENDS

It was now very late and the Jupiter
Troop slowly shuffled back to their tents.
Ms. Bickleblorb looked at Polly.
"I have room in my tent," she said.
Polly looked at Tina and Trudy.
Trudy put her arm around Polly.
"She is fine with us," she said.

"I thought you didn't like me," said Polly.

"I'm sorry I was mean to you," said Trudy. "But when you thought I was in danger you tried to save me. Thank you."

Tina hugged her sister. She was happy Trudy had done the right thing.

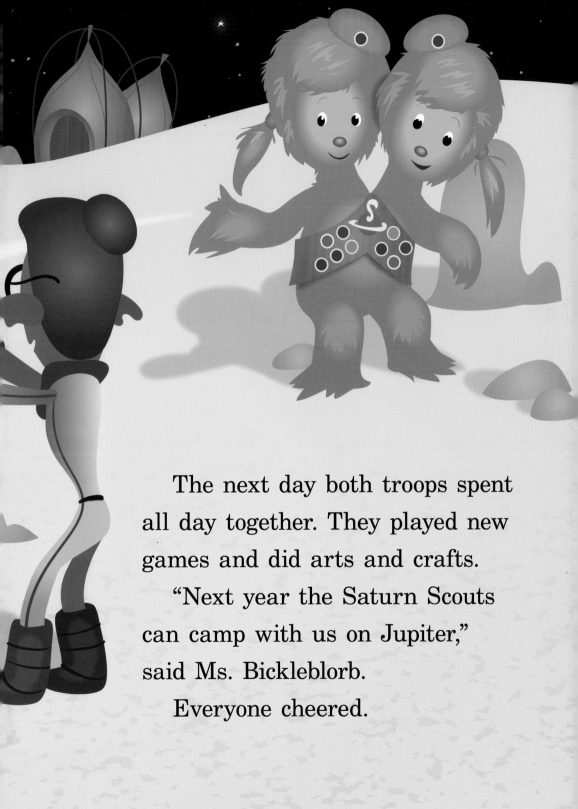

The next day both troops spent
all day together. They played new
games and did arts and crafts.

"Next year the Saturn Scouts
can camp with us on Jupiter,"
said Ms. Bickleblorb.

Everyone cheered.

When it was time to ride the space
bus back home, Tina and Trudy made
room in their seat for their new friend.